First published 2012 by Macmillan Children's Books
This edition published 2013 by Macmillan Children's Books
a division of Macmillan Publishers Limited
20 New Wharf Road, London N1 9RR
Basingstoke and Oxford. Associated companies throughout the world
www.panmacmillan.com
ISBN: 978-0-330-51841-3
Text and illustrations copyright © Chloë Inkpen and Mick Inkpen 2012
Moral rights asserted. All rights reserved.
1 3 5 7 9 8 6 4 2
A CIP catalogue record for this book is available from the British Library.
Printed in China

Pants on the Moon!

Zoe and Beans

Chloë & Mick Inkpen

MACMILLAN CHILDREN'S BOOKS

One windy Thursday
while Zoe was hanging
out her pants to dry,
a **huge** gust of wind
blew across the garden and . . .

. . . whoosh!

Zoe's dress inflated
like a balloon and she
flew up into the air!

Ping! went the washing line.

'Help!' squealed Zoe.

Ping! went the washing line again.

'Grab hold Beans! We're going up!'

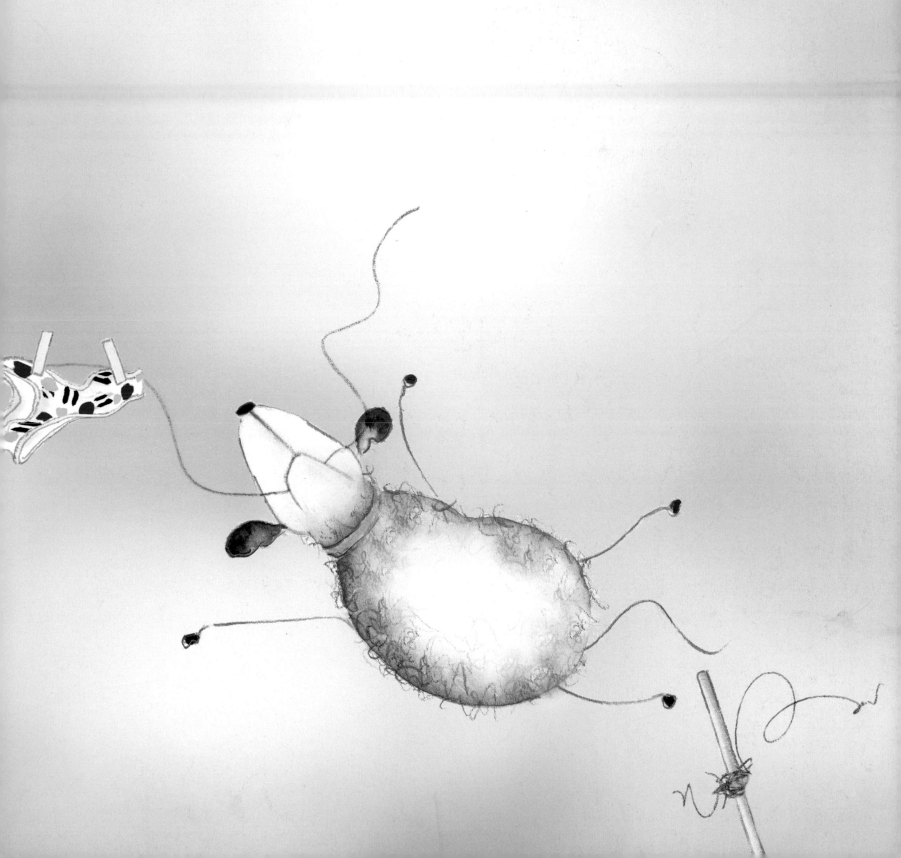

Up went Zoe.
Up went the pegs
  and the pants
    and the washing line.
Up went Beans.
Up they floated.
Up into the blue sky.
Up above the town.
Up, up, up into the
clouds. . .

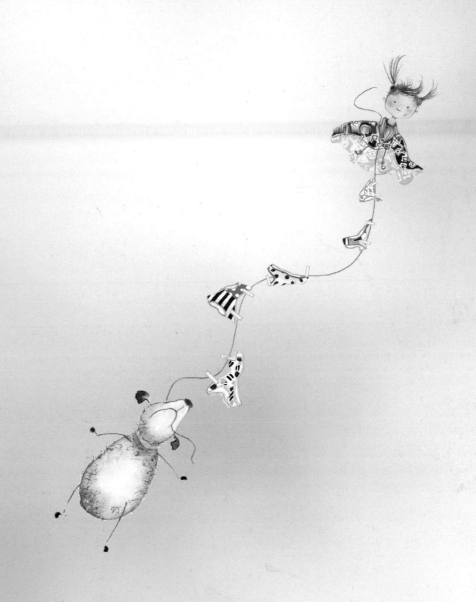

Suddenly there was

a terrible

rushing

rumbling

roari

ng...

ooosh!

The big stinky aeroplane
blew Zoe's dress right off!
It grabbed the washing
line and **hurled** them
into space!

And they landed with a
bump on the moon!

Ouch!
Now Zoe had a
sore bottom,
and her nice clean
pants were covered
in moon dust!

But it's difficult to
stay upset when Beans
is licking your face and
making you giggle...

. . . especially when there's a whole **MOON** to explore!

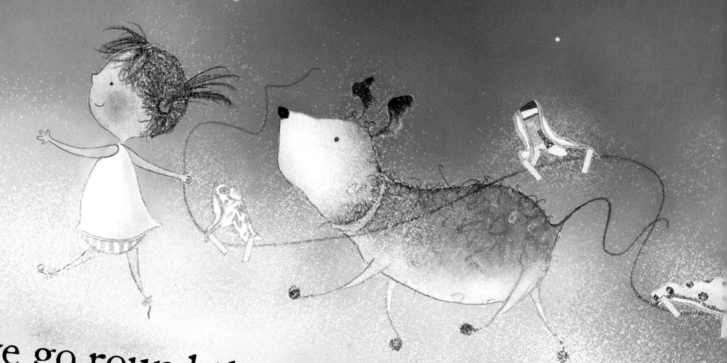

'Here we go round the moony moon. Here we g

They skipped
all the way to
the dark side of
the moon where
they had an
upside-down party
with a moony mole.

Then they skipped all the way back again and bumpe

nto . . .

. . .an odd thing.
'Look Beans!
Somebody's put a **flag**
on the moony moon!'

Zoe and Beans
lay down to catch their
breath, and looked up
at the stars while Zoe
(clever Zoe!) thought of
a way to get back
home. . .

'Goodbye moony moon!'
'Goodbye moony mole!'

They rescued
Zoe's dress on the way
back down . . .

. . . and avoided the stinky aeroplanes.

They crashed into the garden in a big tangly heap.

'Home again!'

said Zoe.

Zoe hummed to herself
as she washed the moondust
out of her pants.

It was long past bedtime
before she was finished.
But **at last** all her pants
were clean . . .

. . . well, nearly all of them.